I0517380

# Rescue Plan

### Stephanie Barbé Hammer

BAMBOO
DART
PRESS

LOS ANGELES † NEW YORK † LONDON † SYDNEY

*Rescue Plan* by Stephanie Barbé Hammer

ISBN: 978-1-947240-09-4

eISBN: 978-1-947240-10-0

Copyright © 2021 Stephanie Barbé Hammer. All rights reserved.

First Printing 2021

For information:

Bamboo Dart Press

chapbooks@bamboodartpress.com

Curated and operated by Dennis Callaci and Mark Givens

Bamboo Dart Press 004

www.pelekinesis.com

www.bamboodartpress.com

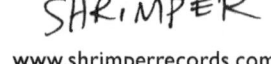
www.shrimperrecords.com

*For Robert F. Gross*

# Advance Reviews

"Gomer Faithcutt is a gentle hero and a noble survivor. He likes swimming and he likes boys and he also likes girls and he needs his father to get back to painting and he needs to stop lying about himself. Most of all, he needs to pass the test to become a junior lifeguard. In *Rescue Plan*, Stephanie Barbé Hammer gives us a delightful tale of friendship and strength and just a splash of magic, all bundled together with warmth and plain talk that feels exactly like wisdom."

**Ana Maria Spagna**, UPLAKE

\* \* \*

"*Rescue Plan* is a gorgeously written and relevant magical story about Gomer, a 15-year-old protagonist who we immediately love and root for as he begins to come of age—unpacking his bisexual identity but also connections to the historical past of the town of Narrow Interior in characters only he can see. We immediately relate to his quest to find his unique strengths under the backdrop of a cancer remission and through his childhood loss of his mother. This book is a delightful, engaging must-read for adults and young adults and will leave you craving to know more about where Gomer's unfolding journeys might take him next and who he might further become."

**Marie Hartung**, National Bisexual Book Award Judge
and author

\* \* \*

"In Gomer Faithcutt, the protagonist of *Rescue Plan*, Stephanie Barbé Hammer has captured all the disorienting, funny, resilient, multi-faceted, wise beyond one's years, awkward complexity of being a 15-year-old in 2020. Both Gomer and the world he inhabits—the aptly named New England town of Narrow Interior—elude neat descriptions and categories: they are self-contained and expansive, conservative and cosmopolitan, populated by nice old ladies and philanthropic celebrity billionaires, and troubled by intolerant histories and uncertain futures. In a queer coming of age story that eschews so many of the tropes of the queer coming of age story, *Rescue Plan* shows a young man reckoning with the distance between dreams and reality, between the desire to rescue others and the necessity to put on your own life jacket first."

**Christopher Records**, author of *Care: Stories*

\* \* \*

"Stephanie Barbé Hammer's stories are often strange, and always a delight. *Rescue Plan* tugs at the film between this world and the shadow of its past inhabitants, and wades through the waters of sickness, health, faith, and self-determination. I am in love with the clip of this story, with the protagonist Gomer Faithcutt—a boy who knows (and sees) things—and the way Hammer has rendered his interior landscape. I love that she grafts together anabaptists ghosts and a queer teen as each search, not necessarily for salvation, but for the rites of passage that will allow them to become themselves."

**Samantha Updegrave**, essayist

\* \* \*

# Rescue Plan

G omer Faithcutt liked swimming. The feeling of weight-lessness. The power to do things he could never do on the ground: somersaults—back and front—handstands, and dives from the highest board. Then, he had started learning to save people from drowning a year ago, last spring. He'd completed the class work for Junior Lifeguard and even taken the written test.

Then he got brain cancer.

Now he would finish this summer at the Narrow Interior Municipal Pool.

**Going to the pool?** Mackie texted him; she was one of his best friends—a girl.

He didn't answer, because, the truth was he preferred walking to the pool alone.

He liked thinking about what he was going to see there.

All winter, the water polo team from the high school up at Amherst had been using the pool for practice, and these boys were tall and powerful, and their legs were muscled to the point of ropiness. And grownup guys came too—policemen and firefighters from Narrow Interior. They used the pool for strength training, and for relaxation. The way those bodies moved through space with ease and knowledge. He wanted to be close to bodies like that.

Gomer knew what coming out was. He had taken the sex-ed

classes, and there were gay people in his town, but they tended to come for weekends and the summer, because they had jobs in the city. They were rich gay people, in other words, and he went to public school, and the local people were different.

And, no, he couldn't tell his father. He'd gotten a sense for what could go wrong with that telling, when he saw that old *X-Men* movie, where the ice-kid tries to tell his parents he can freeze stuff. People say they want to know things, but in the end they don't want to know what they think they do.

He knew too about the queer kids who committed suicide. He was only 15, but he wasn't an idiot. He wasn't going to offer himself up to Mr. Death just yet. His cancer almost killed him once.

The plan was: stay silent; survive.

Did Mackie know? He suspected she suspected. She would almost say, "dude, that's so gay," and then catch herself.

But there was another reason he was interested in the pool. There was something else in the showers.

A woman. That seemed strange given what his proclivities almost certainly were. And yes, he knew the word *proclivities.* He was really smart, but because of his illness he did not skip 9th grade. Thank God. He was already shorter and skinnier than a lot of the boys in his class. He could not have faced 11th grade this past year. Bad enough it was coming up in September.

But yes, he'd seen a woman standing under the shower. A woman who had long hair, wearing a long grey dress. She was almost a trick of the water, the fluorescents shining oddly on the tile.

*My name is Molly*, the almost water woman whispered in the spray of droplets. Unless that was the old pipes whistling through the swim gym building.

Mackie texted him again. **Pool?**

Gomer hadn't told Mackie about the—vision. That made 2 secrets he couldn't share. Gay was bad enough, but the seeing of the almost woman thing?

**NO** he texted, but as he did that, Mackie's own text came in.

**COMING OVER**

"Shit," he said out loud. He liked Mackie. He more than liked her. And that was confusing. How many more than "likes" were there?

Apparently, a lot.

He put his red regulation swim trunks in his Junior Lifeguard bag, and he took the bag with him down the stairs to the faded yellow kitchen. His father, Gideon, was standing on the top rung of a ladder, digging through the cabinets above the refrigerator, pulling out vases and oddly shaped glassware as he yelled across the hall to his boss/landlord in the family room.

"Sylvia—there's no room in here for the vintage juice glasses you bought online," he shouted.

Sylvia was the widow of a geology professor from the college in town—and she was a packrat and now had such bad arthritis, she couldn't really go out, so purchasing online was both a blessing (she got to chat with the seller on e-bay) and a curse (infinite amounts of junk).

Gomer and Gideon had lived with her 5 years. Gideon took care of her and did other chores. That way he could be home for Gomer and have still have the space to be an artist.

But he hadn't made art in months.

"Are you going to paint today?" Gomer asked Gideon as his father came down from the ladder.

"No time," said his father.

"Dad," said Gomer. "You say that every day."

"And every day it's true," said his father. Gideon sat at the kitchen table, lit a cigarette, and looked at his son.

Father and son resembled each other, but not completely. Gideon and Gomer had pale blue eyes, but Gomer had black hair like his mother.

"You shouldn't smoke," said Gomer.

Gideon stubbed out the cigarette. "I'll smoke outside," he said, "so the carcinogens can't get you."

"But they'll get **you**," said Gomer. "Gideon."

Sometimes, when things got serious, Gomer called his father by his first name. Like a lot of people in this town, they both had Bible names, although Gideon wasn't religious, and Gomer's mother, Ming Ming, was a Confucian atheist like most PRC nationals. After the divorce, Gideon made Gomer go to the church near the college. He had heard the coffee ladies muttering about an acquaintance's son who lived in the big city with his—the ladies muttered—BOYFRIEND.

They complained about that when they weren't complaining about how all the manufacturing jobs had gone from Narrow Interior to China.

Gomer wondered. What would it **be** like to live in an apartment in China with one of the firefighters? Who would cook? He supposed the older guy would. In return, Gomer would rescue the firefighter, if he ever fell into the water, because a lot of Chinese people can't swim.

Of course—being gay in China was harder than here, supposedly.

Then he remembered and pulled a crumpled piece of paper out of his gym bag.

"I am going to retest for Junior Lifesaving, Dad," he said. "I need you to sign the slip."

"Buddy," said Gideon, "are you strong enough to take on this kind of physical activity?"

"Dad," said Gomer. "The doctor says I am fine."

"But you can't be too careful," said his father, standing up, and going back to his chores. He always said "you can't be too careful" in a way that drove Gomer crazy.

The kitchen screen door creaked open, and Mackie came through it. She was carrying a towel and her red bathing suit straps peeked from under her underwear shirt. She was tall, and had coppery hair.

Gomer felt a rush of something when he saw her.

"You can't be –" began Gideon for a second time.

"You worry too much, Mr. Faithcutt," said Mackie. She winked at Gomer. She knew the drill.

"The permission slip, Dad," said Gomer.

Gideon sighed and signed. Then he pulled out the frying pan to make up his signature French toast.

"Who wants a spectacular breakfast?" he proclaimed.

"Could I have noodles instead?' Gomer asked. "Like they make in Shanxi Province?"

"Gomer—" said Gideon. "You know I can't make those."

Gomer shrugged. His mother had told him that Shanxi Province was the homeland of 100 different kinds of noodles. When she and Gideon separated, she had gone back there. To take care of her grandmother, who was too old to travel.

She had never come back.

"What a horrible country," the church ladies said. "You can't even get on Google! It's forbidden!"

"French toast is so tasty," interjected Mackie. "Who eats noodles for breakfast anyway?"

"No one eats bread in China," Gomer told her.

"What about all those McDonald's over there, dopey?" she said. She leaned back in her chair and crossed her arms.

"That's just for tourists."

"Who'd want to go to China, anyway?"

"I do," said Gomer.

Gideon slid the slices onto plates. Clanked them down on the table.

"Oh yeah," said Mackie, picking up her fork. "I forgot."

Gomer's mom had left 5 years ago, and a lot of people didn't remember her. And people tend to assume you're just one thing. Not more.

But the French toast was terrific. Gomer ate his slowly, savoring. Mackie ate hers fast and then plunged her fork into Gomer's portion, periodically grabbing a sliver that glistened with maple syrup.

Gideon asked her, "Do you want another slice?"

Mackie licked her fingers and recommenced her not so stealthy attack on unattended French toast fragments. "No thanks—I'd rather steal," she said.

Gomer smiled. Mackie was direct. He liked that.

The kitchen door creaked open a second time.

"Gomer?" said a plaintive child's voice.

"Come on in Birdie!" said Gideon.

Mackie's younger sister Birdie wandered in, wearing an already dirty lavender dress.

"Gomer, come play Playmobil with me!" she said, ignoring both her sister and Gideon.

"What are you doing walking across the street by yourself?" said Mackie. She stood up, ready to play her favorite role—Responsible Older Sister.

"Gamera walked with me," Birdie said.

Mackie rolled her eyes. "Oh God, not that again."

Birdie's latest obsession was a radioactive giant turtle of post WW2 Japanese science fiction. She had seen some of the old Mystery Science Theater 3000 movies that Mackie's parents were watching. Now it was all Gamera all the time.

"Gamera has special powers," Birdie said. "Maybe I'll tell you—" she pointed at Gomer. "But not you—" she stuck her tongue out at her sister. "'cause you never believe me, when I tell you stuff."

Mackie turned to Gomer and his father.

"I'd better get her back home, before my mom has a nervous breakdown."

"See you at the pool—" said Gomer.

Mackie put her hands on her sister's shoulders and started propelling her out the door.

"You know what?" said Birdie hopping on one foot and then the other.

"Birdie come ON," said Mackie.

"The water taught me a song!" cried Birdie, and as Mackie opened the door she sang out: "'Dollies dollies for our Molly. She's got the secret light by golly.'"

"What song is that?" Said Gomer.

"Who knows?" said Mackie.

Birdie kept on singing as the kitchen door creaked open and slammed. Out the window, above the sink, Gomer could see Birdie dancing on the curb of Green Street, while Mackie gesticulated, pointing left then right in what was clearly an effort to explain the watch-for-ongoing-traffic principle.

Gomer chuckled. Birdie had something of a crush on him—or whatever it is that 5-year-olds feel for someone older. She gave him a cheap Barbie doll knock off once with red hair that she'd gotten at the 99 Cent store.

"You need a friend," she had said to him. "The dollies can be magic."

He still had the Barbie. He had taken it with him to the hospital. Along with the GI Joe action figure, that had been his father's.

Now, something made him go back upstairs.

He noticed that his heart pounded as he ran up the stairs. He was out of shape.

He walked into his bedroom.

He got the dolls out and made them jump up and down on top of the dresser.

"Remember Jacob?" Barbie said to GI Joe.

When Gomer was in the cancer ward, there was this kid, Jacob, who was a bit younger than him. His father was Korean and his parents were divorced too. The two patients hung out. Jacob became blind, which was bad because he was a World of Warcraft fanatic, and near the end Gomer was working the controls for him, and telling him what was happening to his character.

Then Jacob died. He was 13. He hadn't done anything wrong, but he was dead all the same. And no one seemed to know that he had Asian heritage, except for Gomer.

"People make stupid assumptions!" said GI Joe to Barbie.

"I hate these stereotypes," she said back to him.

"Gomer," called his father. "Don't you need to get to the pool?"

Gomer threw the dolls back into the top drawer. He ran down the stairs.

Once there, he could hear drawers opening and closing, closet doors being opened and shut as his father continued to argue with his boss about what they should throw away.

"I might need those turquoise plastic dessert dishes!" Sylvia explained. Gideon sighed loudly.

"All right, but you could please put out one of these cigarettes? You've got two burning in the ashtray."

Sylvia was a chain smoker which made Gideon smoke more.

*I need to get him to stop*, Gomer thought. He walked outside.

The sky was overcast, and the air was unseasonably cold. The wind came up and whispered at him.

Birdie and Mackie were still standing in Sylvia's driveway, their eyes fastened on something going on across the street.

Across the street there was a moving van, and next to that a lady in an apron yelling in a strange language at a guy in a pink shirt wrestling with another guy wearing—whatever it is that the Dalai Lama wears. Only he was young, kind of chubby, and he had a cigar jammed between his teeth.

"Stop spying on me on behalf of Holbein Hotels," yelled the guy in the pink shirt," as he gave the Dalai Lama man a hard shove. "I don't need your help."

"Dude," said the Dalai Lama guy, after he fell down and got back up. "You so *do* need me to help with the building restoration."

*Stop fighting,* the wind whispered.

Gomer looked around. No one else heard, and the fight continued.

He looked at his phone. The Junior Lifeguard certification class! He was running late.

"I got to go," he said, but Mackie grabbed his arm.

"Shouldn't we—I don't know—call the police or get a grown-up?"

"Go get *your* parents," said Gomer.

"My dad is at the restaurant and my mom has to deal with Birdie. Go get your dad."

"He's busy," said Gomer.

Mackie looked at him.

"He is right here in the HOUSE!" she said.

"He's busy," said Gomer.

The 2 men were now wrestling on the driveway, each one trying to pin the other to the cement.

"Then why don't *we* do something?" Mackie said.

"Because we are just kids, and we aren't supposed to, like, *get involved* in adult ... disputes." What he said sounded stupid even though it was true.

"See you at the pool then," she replied. She turned her back and hurried Birdie across the street.

"I just don't want to be late," he called after her.

"So don't be," she said.

As Gomer traipsed down the street, he turned briefly to look at the fighting men. They punched each other, then stopped, and lay side by side on the driveway, gazing up at the sky.

Gomer walked quickly past the now quiet houses. Past the athletic fields of the college, past Geister Woods, past Pardonme Creek.

The wind whispered at him.

*Dollies dollies for our Molly*

He got to the pool, and went into the locker room. It was empty, and he could hear the echo of boys and girls already at the pool, and the faint whistle of the swimming coach.

There was water dripping from one of the showers. Gomer threw on his trunks, and looked.

The water drops shimmered.

*Through water I make my truth known.*

He wanted to stay, but there was no time.

The swimming instructor glared when Gomer showed up pool-side. Coach Birch was one of those typical lifeguard guys: tall, muscled, blonde.

But there was nothing beautiful about him. He had no grace.

"Faithcutt!" yelled the coach. "What's your excuse for coming into the pool facility 15 minutes late?"

"There was a fight on the street in front of my house," Gomer said.

There were some *woah's* and *wtf's* from the other students. Gomer saw Mackie standing silently in the shallow end (how the heck had she managed to get there on time?)

The coach silenced them.

"Were you attacked and therefore needed to defend yourself?" he asked.

"No." said Gomer. The other kids looked at each other. Where was this line of questioning going?

"Were you the attacker?" Giggles and guffaws at that. Gomer's general nerdiness was well known at school and at church.

"No."

"Well" said the coach. "Did you intervene and stop the fight?" He paused, waiting for the answer.

Mackie raised her eyebrows with an *I told you so* arch to them.

Gomer looked at the pool, and inhaled the extreme chlorination fumes that rose from its depths, because Mr. Wayne, the janitor was convinced that a lot of chlorination would keep away sexually transmitted diseases.

He thought about explaining that the combatants were grown men, and he was a kid.

But he could see that, like Mackie, the coach seemed to think that he, Gomer, OUGHT to have done something.

"No." he said. "I didn't do anything."

The coach, let out a hissing breath like air escaping from a balloon. "If you can't behave like a responsible citizen or like a man, then you can at least show up here on time," he said.

"I'm sorry?" said Gomer, the sentence emerging from his lips like a suggestion.

"Pussy," said some boy next to him, although Gomer was sure he would have done exactly the same thing.

"Get in and swim 20 laps," said the coach. "Freestyle."

"The rest of you—let's talk about the principles of water safety. Look at the items on the whiteboard—"

Gomer clearly remembered the basics of water safety around a swimming pool, so he got in the water and started turning his ear towards the water, and back. Turn breath, stroke, stroke. Again.

He heard the truncated words of the coach reading off the white board:

"Don't-fly-kite-near –in – g-pool."

1 lap. 2 laps. 3 laps. 4 laps.

He was getting tired.

He heard a whistle.

"Faithcutt!"

He saw the coach waving him over to the side of the pool. The coach crouched down, and glared at him.

"What are you—an old man?" Said the coach. "Speed up. You're swimming like a turtle." He looked up "Isn't he, guys?" Laughter. The coach smiled.

*Nice work, coach. Brutalize one guy and ask the others to think it funny.*

He never understood this maneuver. Perhaps that's why he had no male friends.

Neither did his dad.

6 laps. 9 laps. 14 laps. 15 laps. He saw Mackie's legs briefly with the long scar running up the thigh. From that time she tried tightrope walking, and fell on a fence.

Whistle.

"We can't wait all day for you to finish your laps, Faithcutt," said the coach. "You'll have to come in early tomorrow to do the rest." He turned to the class.

"All right everyone, now work in pairs and come up with 5 safety issues, fill out these worksheets, and then we'll look at a video about the real deal—open water lifeguarding at the beach."

Gomer hoisted himself up out of the pool with difficulty. He'd need to train hard now to get stronger.

The class filled out the worksheets and handed them in. As they watched the video that focused on flags and what they meant at the beach (not that they lived anywhere near an ocean), the Senior Lifeguard class appeared.

The Junior lifeguard class watched as the almost adult looking 16-18 year old people came poolside.

Unlike Coach Birch, the Senior Lifeguard instructor looked cheerful and kind, with braids twisted back away from her face and a smile that looked pretty genuine.

Next to her walked a student with a chain around his neck.

A week ago Gomer had interrupted his father and Sylvia watching a weird movie about an old man who dyed his hair really black sitting on a beach chair in Venice watching a boy in the ocean. The movie really *was* kind of gay, but Gideon said it was based on a famous story, and could he, Gomer, please just let him, Gideon, concentrate. The boy in the movie was a spindly and uninteresting, but this guy at the pool—he was someone you'd want to watch from the position of a beach chair. For a long time.

Not tall, but somehow graceful, he moved through space in this completely relaxed way. He wore an old retro plaid red swimming suit that had numbers on it like something from the 50's. He had longish curly brown hair.

The boy noticed Gomer looking at him. He smiled a big smile, and waved.

Gomer looked away. Then he looked back. The guy was still smiling. Gomer tried to smile back, but it felt like his teeth got stuck on his upper lip and he kind of gaped instead.

"Faithcutt—what does a—flag mean?"

Jesus—Gomer hadn't been listening, and didn't have a clue, but the Senior Lifeguard coach saved him, shouting:

"Yo Birch—it's our turn for the pool!"

They all got out. The coach drew him aside.

""Show up early tomorrow morning," he said, "and don't try that bullshit 'oooh I've been sick' junk. This is IMPORTANT training. Get your act together."

Gomer's head retracted into the beach towel lying on his shoulders.

He walked down to the locker room and got dressed. When he came out of the building, Mackie was there, talking in a very loud, enthusiastic voice with the handsome older boy.

"Hey Gomer, this is Christopher; he just moved here from Holyoke," said Mackie, her eyes shining.

Before he could speak, Christopher stuck out his hand.

"Hey Gomer," he said. "What a great name that is!"

"Aren't you supposed to be in practice?" was all he could say. *Great*, he thought, *I sound like someone's mom.*

Christopher nodded seriously. "For sure, but Coach Elam sent me out because she's expecting some equipment that her husband is bringing over from Red Cross headquarters."

Mackie beamed at him.

"Do you hope to get, like, a job as a lifeguard over the summer if you can get certified in time?" she asked.

*Damn*, thought Gomer, *now that's an intelligent question!*

"Maybe," said Christopher. "I—" he looked at the two younger kids. "I mean this is really cool and all, but—"

Gomer spoke suddenly. "You have other interests."

Christopher laughed and scratched his curly mop of hair.

"Word," he said. "I *have a lot* of other interests, but my mom and my Parole Officer say I need to do activities that will demonstrate my—"

"You were in JAIL?" Mackie breathed out. Her mouth opened with shock and fascination.

Christopher nodded. "Armed Robbery –" he said. "But I was tried as a juvenile, and went to—"

"Like juvenile detention?" Gomer said.

"It was more like a hospital," said Christopher.

"Hospitals are hell," said Gomer.

"That, they are." Christopher said.

A car swung over with the trunk half-open.

"Hey kids," said the driver. "I've got the rescue tubes for Coach Elam's class."

Christopher waved at the man. He turned to Mackie and Gomer.

"Good to meet you both. See you at the pool!" he said. He ran over to the car.

Mackie talked all the way home about Christopher. Every sentence ended with "isn't he cool?" Gomer repeated the word "cool" in the small gaps in the conversation.

"Uh Oh—" said Mackie, as they turned onto their street.

A news van was parked in front of the house where the moving truck had been, and just a little ahead of them, was one of the combatants—the guy in the pink shirt, standing at entrance to the driveway. A mob of 20 or 30 people stood scrunched up on the front porch, and they were all asking him questions at the same time.

"Henry Holbein—we want to know what brings you to Narrow Interior!" shouted a woman who got out of the van, as two cameramen walked up the driveway with her towards the guy—Henry. The people on the porch stopped yelling questions. They came down the driveway til the man in the pink was surrounded.

Gideon came out of the house to survey the goings on.

"Who is that man?" said Mackie.

"I think," said Gideon, "that's the billionaire who's come to build a new hotel downtown. Let's go inside."

Henry Holbein the hotel billionaire stood stiffly on the driveway with the reporter, the cameras, and the onlookers. He was short and slender, and he jumped slightly whenever the cameras moved.

"Wow—I'm going to go home and tell Mom that we have a billionaire in the neighborhood," said Mackie.

Gomer went inside, yelled hi to Sylvia, and went upstairs into his bedroom where he had a good view of the goings on at the front of the house across the street. The interview seemed to go on forever. More people kept on arriving, and at one point a pizza delivery car came; the guy got out with about 20 boxes. That's when Henry invited the whole crowd into the house for pizza.

*He ordered pizzas for all these people?* thought Gomer. *He must be really rich.*

There was no sign of the Dalai Lama guy with the cigar. Perhaps he had been beaten into submission after Gomer left, although he tended to doubt it.

Later that evening, Gomer reheated the macaroni and cheese that Gideon had made and listened to Gideon serving Sylvia supper and asking her about a cache of depression glass butter dishes that had been uncovered in the attic.

"Sylvia," Gideon said. "That's the 4th cigarette you've left burning on the edge of your desk—you're going to burn the house down one of these days."

Gomer went back upstairs. He wanted to think about Christopher. He lay on the bed—and thought.

That night he dreamed of the woman in the old-fashioned grey dress.

*Look for the light within*, Molly told him. She stroked his hair from his forehead like his mother used to. *The divine is here between people who love each other.* Christopher bent over from the other side, and stroked his forehead too.

But then the dream went bad. There were monsters in a hospital. They were doctors and they were patients too. And they surrounded him with enormous eyes and cartoon clown faces. *You will die and you'll be trapped here with us*, they all shout. He could feel the radiation treatments burning the flesh off his bones.

*You'll die forever,* they said. *You'll just keep dying.*

He awakened. The moon was out. He went to the window.

Outside across the street, someone was sitting on the front steps. The porch light was on and Gomer could see that it was Henry Holbeln. He had his head in his hands.

Gomer stood at the window. He waited but Henry Holbein did not look up.

He slept.

Gomer went downstairs for breakfast.

Gideon was hunched over the landline in the yellow kitchen.

"Yes," said Gideon.

An hour later Gomer and his father sat in the doctor's waiting room.

His cell phone buzzed and the pasty looking adults and kids who sat in the room looked at him mournfully.

A text from Mackie:

**where are you?** she wrote. **the coach is going to kill you!**

what to say?

*no problem—something else will kill me first*

or

*I'm dead anyway?*

He texted simply

**at the doctor's**

**Shit** was the reply.

The fakely cheerful nurse in the pink smock called his name.

"Hi Gomer," she said brightly. "Good to see you."

"Your markers are up, my friend," the doctor said. "We're going to do more tests ...."

Then he got all encouraging and said things like "we need to see what's happening so we can nail this thing."

The unsaid C-word hung in the air.

Gideon started asking questions in a monotone voice that Gomer hated. Gomer looked at the clock on the doctor's desk.

"Dad," said Gomer. "You need to contact the coach about the Junior Lifesaving class."

"Buddy," said Gideon. "I really don't think—"

"Great idea!" said the doctor brightly—can a voice be falsely bright? "In fact, Gomer, I will write you a note to give to the coach."

"It's good to follow a regular schedule and pursue regular activities," he said to Gideon. "It helps recovery to have a positive attitude."

*Jesus*, thought Gomer. *Why can't adults understand how to talk to kids?*

"I'd like to talk with your father about a billing question, Gomer," said the doctor. "So why don't you go outside for a second."

"Fine," said, Gomer. He thought for a moment. "Dad—If we hurry, I might be able to catch the coach before the afternoon swim session, and I can at least get my extra laps in."

"Gomer, please," said his father. he looked grey and aged and rumpled and pained. "Please try to be patient, buddy."

*I fucking hate that expression*, he thought.

He pulled the door open, walked out of the doctor's office. Walked through the waiting room past the still frightened faces, and got outside.

He alternated walking and running—his gym bag slamming against his ribs—in the direction of the municipal pool.

By the time Gomer arrived, Coach Birch was doing the advanced Senior lifeguard training—Coach Elam was out sick—and he looked less than thrilled to see Gomer standing at the poolside.

"Get out," he said curtly. "You were absent for the second time, and you didn't handle your extra laps. I won't have this kind of attitude on my team."

"Please," said Gomer, "Coach, Mr. Birch— I need to speak with you."

He got sent to the office, where he waited a good hour.

He listened to the echoing voices, and whistle, and the slapping of bodies against the water. The sound of swimming. It soothed.

His mother had taught him how to swim.

"It's a real power," she had told him. "Float and survive." Then, she showed him how to lie on top of the water. Letting it lift you up. Carry you.

"Now—" she said. "Let's see you hold your breath and open your eyes underwater. Let's see you swim as far as you can underwater." She believed in him. She knew he could do it.

*Dwe-bu-chi,* she had whispered in his ear, when she got on the shuttle to go to the airport.

*I'm sorry.*

He was 9.

Swimming was a way to be close to her and to that feeling of *you can do it.* If someone you love teaches you something—anything— it's a gift you hold on to. It's a raft and a buoy. It's a life-preserver.

Gomer closed his eyes.

"Wake up Faithcutt—what do you want?"

Coach Birch finally appeared and sat down at the old metal desk that served as the office. He glared at Gomer. Under the fluorescent lights the Coach's tan looked fake and his hair appeared to be dyed.

"I have a doctor's note."

28

The coach held his hand out, took the note and read it.

"So?" he said.

At least he didn't do what other adults did—get all embarrassed and/or fake sympathetic.

"I want to take the test," Gomer said.

The coach snorted and shook his head. "You haven't even done a week of the class work."

"But I have," said Gomer. "Remember? I finished it last spring before I got sick." He leaned forward.

"Can't you waive a repeat of the classwork, and let me take the test early—in case I get too sick to do it?"

"I don't think you're up to it," the coach said flatly. He stood up.

"Then let me fail it," said Gomer.

The coach looked at him. He lifted his chin.

"If you flunk, you flunk. No appeals."

"Correct, sir," said Gomer.

"Two weeks," said the Coach.

"What?"

"Noon, the Monday after next—some Senior Lifeguard students will test at that time too."

Gomer's heart pounded when he walked down to the showers. What the hell was he doing?

*I'm an idiot. I can't get ready that fast.*

It was raining in the locker room.

The shower furthest to the left had sprung multiple leaks and was spraying water from the nozzle head and from the main pipe that connected to the other showers. There was water coming from different directions. The spray came together, became a torrent, and the torrent solidified, took form and as he watched, he saw her—the woman—the woman he'd seen before. A woman in grey materialized in the center of the room, her long hair streaming down, and there was a man with her in a white shirt and they were laughing.

Birdie's song played in his head.

*Molly?* He thought.

*Yes, friend,* said the water-woman as she turned to him. *And this is Bernhard.*

Gomer could feel his heart pounding faster and faster.

*Er versteht uns nicht,* said the man; he seemed to shimmer in the rising steam.

*We are the Dankers,* she said. *Our meeting places are here. Because the water is here.*

*Wir taufen,* said the man.

"What language is that?" Gomer said.

They extended their hands to Gomer.

*Only adults can choose the light by immersion.*

*Will you choose?* Molly said. Or else it was the water pounding on the floor.

Without even meaning to, Gomer lifted his arms.

Then he heard something he hadn't heard the other times. A stringed instrument was being plucked delicately, and behind the couple made up of water Gomer could almost see other human figures in black moving, holding objects he couldn't quite distinguish.

He kept his hands stretched out as he walked towards the water people.

Then the locker room revolved around Gomer and he felt himself falling.

Someone caught him, just before he hit his head on the cement floor.

"Hey dude, are you ok?"

It was the handsome guy, Christopher.

He had his arms around him. "You were standing there staring into space, muttering, and then you started to sway."

Christopher stood him back up, and Gomer pulled away and walked over to his locker. He could feel himself turning red.

"I just felt dizzy for a second," said Gomer.

"It's probably your blood sugar," said Christopher, sitting on the bench. "Swimming really drains you so you have to eat a clean diet."

"Yeah, I'm tired." Gomer took a breath and looked at Christopher. The older boy smiled, chill as ever.

"Hey  " he said, pointing at one of the showers. "What were you staring at?"

"Did you hear any music?" Gomer asked, changing the subject.

"That was me," said Christopher, and nodded at a black case lying open beside him on the bench. Inside was an instrument that looked like a small, pear-shaped guitar.

"Sometimes I get ideas," Christopher said. "Then I have to stop and play the ideas so as not to lose the music."

"You know," said Gomer. "I *do* feel kind of hungry."

"Let's get something to eat!" Christopher replied.

They put their clothes on. Gomer tried not to look at Christopher, and failed, while the older boy talked about swimming and nutrition.

They walked out of the swim gym and Christopher pointed out his moped.

"This isn't a motorcycle," said Christopher. "But we can get around faster than walking, that's for sure."

Gomer got on behind him.

The roads of Narrow Interior were bumpy but Christopher took the bumps and turns easily, as Gomer swayed with him.

It felt to Gomer like he was holding onto a live wire of sinews and energy. No, it was more solid than that. Warmer. Shoulder blades jutting into him as they took the turns together. Back muscles flexing against him. And inside it all, a heart that was beating on the same side as his. Ahead of his. Powering them both forward.

They hit downtown in a matter of minutes and cruised along Main Street, swerving in and out of the tight spaces between the cars. As Christopher maneuvered, Gomer could feel himself easing into the ride, and he followed the movements of the body in front of him. It was a slow dance on wheels.

Christopher glided down Main Street and stopped in front of the Boll Weevil Organic Café and Pizza Shop. FIND YOUR FAVORITE AUTHOR HERE! read a dented, yellow sign above the door.

The Boll Weevil was filled with famous author memorabilia for reasons that no one really understood. Charles Dickens plates and Shakespeare teacups hung from the ceilings and were stacked up along the walls in a clutter of junk.

His father never took him there because the food was this terrible vegan crap. "They don't even use real cheese!" Gideon said once.

Christopher and Gomer walked in, and as the door slammed shut, all the antique plates and memorabilia clanked and clicked.

"Hey Ali," said Christopher to a beautiful boy who grabbed boxes behind the counter, and headed out.

"Hey," said the boy in accented English. "Did you catch Milano versus Manchester?"

"I think Valerie taped it," he said. He turned to Gomer.

"Valerie is my girlfriend."

"Your what?" said Gomer.

"My girlfriend," said Christopher. But—" he sat back. "It's kind of open."

Christopher leaned back, tipping the chair backwards. He looked at Gomer.

"Do you know what bisexual means?"

"Is that a real thing?" said Gomer, before he could stop himself.

"Hell yeah," said Christopher.

One of several waitresses with multiple piercings and purple hair came by to take their order.

Christopher ordered juices and pizza with tofu.

"Tofu fights cancer," said Christopher. "and I'm treating."

"Thanks," said Gomer. "So—does everyone know about my cancer?"

Christopher laughed. "Pretty much." He looked at Gomer. "But, it's ok to tell the truth about yourself."

"Since when?" said Gomer.

"Since always," said Christopher. "If you lie about who you are, you kill yourself a little every day."

Gomer nodded. "I think I'm bisexual, too," he said. "I'm not sure."

Christopher nodded. "Cool."

The drinks came. They both drank.

"How about a song while we're waiting for the pizza?" Gomer noticed then, that Christopher had brought the little black case in with him.

"What kind of guitar is that?" said Gomer.

"It's a mandolin," said Christopher. "An old instrument from the old world."

The authorial dishes rattled on their racks as Christopher tuned the strings, the purple haired waitresses frothed milk for lattes and Ali came back in to pick up another order. He was followed by a goth girl with a huge octopus tattoo on her chest and an older woman wearing a graduation robe and cap.

Christopher started playing. The mandolin had a high sweet quality to it. It sounded like rain drops. Like water playing on your imagination.

Then Christopher began to sing:

*And I roam and I roam and I roam and I search*

*For the wooden house that ain't no church*
*For Molly and her dollies that crossed the sea*
*With Bernhard and the Dankers' company*
*Searching out the light.*

There were many verses to the song, and Gomer didn't follow it all. It was a sad song about getting drunk at a bar and remembering what Narrow Interior had been like in the olden days: how two lovers came here from Europe to worship a different kind of religion—a religion that had a puppet play in it—and they had gotten killed in a fire along with all their friends.

"Here it comes," said Christopher periodically, as the refrain came back. Gomer, tentatively, tried to sing.

Singing was something that Gomer didn't enjoy doing normally, but singing in this group was different. It was like church, or what he imagined church might be, if there wasn't all that stuff about sin and the cross.

The others felt it too. The waitresses sang, the goth girl sang, Ali sang too, and even the lady in the graduation gown, took off her square hat, put it up to her heart and tried it. No one seemed to care who was best and who was worst, who was fastest and who was slowest, who was gay or straight or bisexual or whatever, and who was part something as opposed to part something else. It all dissolved, as the mandolin plucked its heartbreaking notes.

Then Christopher's voice swelled, and the music became more complicated:

*Tell the builders of stone, leave the Dankers alone*
*I heard the wind a'calling*

*Let them perform the play, keep the pastors away*
*The birds sang all night long*
*And I cry to the trees, water rushing at me*
*Tell me where are the friends I'm seeking*
*But the trees won't speak*
*For the place we sought is lost and fallen*
*Still we dream of water again and again*
*Searching out the light...*

Christopher fell silent and the mandolin's strings stilled.

They all sat.

Then the moment passed. The lady with the graduation outfit put her cap back on. The girl with the octopus tattoo talked to one of the waitresses with the purple hair.

"What song is that?" said Gomer.

"It's about the Dankers, the people who founded this town," said Christopher. He lay his mandolin back in its case gently, as though it were a baby or a delicate pet.

The pizza came and it was indeed as terrible as Gideon said. But Gomer thought of the tofu fighting whatever was inside of him, and he ate 3 slices, and drank the green juice Christopher had ordered.

"I wonder sometimes about the builders of stone things in that song," said Christopher.

"Isn't it symbolic?" Gomer said. "I mean like builders who want to make big buildings, like skyscrapers or hotels –"

"Like this guy"—said one of the purple haired waitresses at the bar.

The Boll Weevil had a small but functioning television on the wall. It was on, and Ali turned it up.

**"What does hotel magnate Henry Holbein have planned for Narrow Interior?—News at 5"** said a woman in a business suit.

They finished their pizza and they walked out to the moped.

"Goodbye Christopher!" said Ali.

"I can walk from here," said Gomer.

"Let me take you," said Christopher.

"Isn't your—girlfriend waiting for you?" Gomer said.

"No," said Christopher. He put his hand on Gomer's shoulder.

"Let's go by way of Geister Woods," he said.

And right there on Main Street, in front of the Boll Weevil, Christopher kissed him.

Later that night Gomer lay in bed with Barbie and GI Joe.

They had done a lot of things in the woods. It was strange—having an orgasm—in front of another person. It was hard to do.

And then it wasn't.

The next day the Junior Lifesaving class did some practice testing in the pool with the Senior Lifesaving students, and the coach brought several of his own oversized friends to get in the water and flail like drowning people.

But as Gomer approached a huge suntanned guy, his courage failed him. The man grabbed at him with meaty hands, and Gomer couldn't help it—he swam away as fast as he could.

How do you even deal with a drowning person twice your size?

"Get back over there and save him!" said Coach Birch.

Christopher swam over to him.

"You need to be more aggressive," he said to Gomer. "I'll show you, but I need you and Mackie to help me with something later."

"Sure. What. Do. You need?" Gomer said catching his breath.

"For you both to help me get into the old Danker meetinghouse near the college."

"Why?" Gomer said.

"Because we need to get to something that's there."

"STOP GABBING AND START SWIMMING."

Over the next 2 weeks Coach Birch still gave Gomer hell all the time, but Christopher trained with him during the free swim period—after the Senior Lifesaving class and before the senior citizens and tiny tots hour.

And then they went to the woods.

**Are you done practicing yet?** Mackie texted him every afternoon.

**Nope**. Technically true.

At the pool, Christopher worked him hard, making him do laps with the kick board, using only legs and then holding the kick board between his knees, swimming only with his arms — which was even worse.

But at the end of the first week, Gomer started to swim faster. His body felt stronger.

"You'd make a great lifeguard," he said to Christopher, one afternoon as they lay on the forest floor of Geister Woods. Pardoneme Creek splashed in nearby.

Christopher snorted. "I'll never do anything like that."

"Then—why are you doing this program?" Gomer, turned over and asked him.

"Probation, and also I'm going to need to convince a judge to let me emancipate from my mom," Christopher said.

"What's emancipation?" Gomer asked. Christopher explained.

They stood up, brushed the pine needles off, and rearranged their clothes.

"Why are **you** doing the program?" he said, as Gomer picked up his gym bag.

"I want to be able to save somebody," Gomer answered. They walked over to the moped.

"I felt that way once," said Christopher. "But sometimes your first responsibility is to save yourself. "

"Save myself?" said Gomer. "When would I need to do that?"

"It happens," said Christopher.

They followed this schedule every day.

Practicing got harder. More laps. More information. And on the last practice day, Christopher became the frightening drowner that had so scared Gomer.

Gomer approached the thrashing carefully. But, just when he was figuring out whether to go left or right, Christopher put a long arm out and grabbed him and pulled him under the water.

He wrapped his legs around Gomer's middle, and then sank them both like a stone.

Gomer squirmed but couldn't get loose.

Christopher brought them back up.

"With someone this desperate you have to fight your way out," he said to Gomer.

"Try it."

The next time, Christopher got his arm around his neck and Gomer thought he was going to choke.

They broke away from each other, Gomer gasped for breath and grabbed the edge of the pool.

"Dude, listen to me," said Christopher. "You can't EVER let that happen! You need to slip away by going under water the minute you feel that arm going around your neck."

They kept at it. Gomer kept on drowning. He was getting tired.

Christopher was wearing out also, and he got careless. He poked Gomer in the eye, and threw his arm around his neck—pulling the younger boy towards him in a chokehold. Gomer turned, pulled in his legs and kicked at Christopher.

He got away.

"Better," said Christopher. "Just don't kick me in the balls next time, all right?"

They held on to the edge of the pool.

"I think… I …got this," Gomer said, "if you are there, if you'll be my volunteer victim. We can bring volunteers from the team if we want."

"I'll be there for sure," said Christopher.

"It's tomorrow, remember," Gomer said, pulling himself out of the pool. It was easy to do now. They walked down to the locker room.

"I got you," Christopher said. "But remember, you and me and

Mackie got plans for tonight."

"Can we wait?—I don't want to be too tired for the test."

"It'll be fast but it has to be tonight, because—I—need to get down there."

"To find answers?"

"Yeah—and there's money—gold coins in a box there somewhere."

"Who told you that?"

"A guy I know."

Gomer came very close to saying "this sounds dumb," but he stopped himself.

Instead he asked "Why is Mackie in on this?"

"Because she's skinny and little. You'll see."

They changed clothes.

"You can do things with money." Christopher said. "You could—go to China."

"Not at 15, I can't."

"You don't know what you can do until you try it."

Christopher grabbed his bag.

"I can't go to the woods today." He added "Probation."

Gomer set his alarm for 2 in the morning. He got up, tiptoed down the stairs, and eased himself out the kitchen door. He walked across the street and started crossing yards.

The first yard was the new neighbor's, Henry Holbein. Lights were on, and so Gomer hesitated, but he lined himself up by the hedges and crept. He wasn't fast but he could be silent if he had to be. He walked past the big side window and saw the man Henry walking and moving. He had what looked like a large stuffed animal that he was moving with one arm. The other held a stick to which the left arm was attached. He was showing this animal—it looked like a monkey—to the Dalai Lama guy.

*Neighbors sure are strange*, thought Gomer, as he crept past. The first gate let him into Mackie's backyard. She was waiting with a flashlight. They walked together across Sage Street, and through 2 more backyards. Then they were at the meetinghouse.

Christopher greeted them on his moped. Mackie waved. Without speaking, she slipped through the narrow gap in the gate and the fence. Christopher handed her tools piece by piece as she picked the padlock on the other side.

"How do you guys know how to do that?" Gomer whispered.

Christopher replied—"we've been meeting to practice."

*Why didn't they tell me?*, he thought.

The gate opened and they got through.

"Now, the door," said Christopher softly. He tried it. It too was locked from the inside.

"There's a broken window around the other side," he said. "I've checked. Mackie, you need to climb in. You hold the tools, Gomer."

Mackie disappeared around the back of the house.

"She's a cool girl," said Christopher. "Have you ever thought about —?"

"No," said Gomer holding tightly to the bag and the flashlight.

*Was that true?*

The front door opened.

"There's nothing here," said Mackie. "It's just an empty room."

They walked in. Gomer had expected pews and a pulpit like in the church he went to. They ran their flashlights but all they saw was wood. No chairs even. There were rotted mats on the floor made of something—they smelled.

"What's that?" said Christopher.

"Water," said Gomer. "I hear water dripping towards the back."

They walked carefully. Trying not to stumble on the rotting flooring.

"There's like a cistern here," said Mackie. "A well." They shone their flashlights in what seemed to be a tub of water.

"That's not the dripping water," said Gomer. "It's coming from someplace else."

There was a closet at the back with hooks. The flickering flashlights showed a kind of cupboard.

"It's coming from here," said Gomer.

He tripped on the rotting matting, and pulled one of the hooks to keep himself upright.

The wall creaked and opened.

Stairs.

"The treasure must be down here," Christopher said. He took the stairs.

*There's no treasure here.* thought Gomer.

Still, he followed Christopher and Mackie.

The stone steps led down until they reached a tunnel. They

walked until the tunnel slanted upwards.

They saw light. More steps.

It was a streetlight.

They had emerged at the point where Geister Woods met the road that Christopher took from the pool. They looked back. The stairs faded into the darkness. Pardonme Creek bubbled up along the road.

Mackie was breathing heavily.

"Whoa," she said. "That was scary."

"No buried treasure." Christopher laughed—but Gomer could tell—he sounded upset.

"It's a secret passage," Gomer said. "for the secret religion. That did something with water."

"Whatever," said Christopher.

"Let's go home," Mackie said.

"I have to go back and get my moped," Christopher said. "But it's cool—I'll see you at swimming—ok?"

Gomer walked Mackie home and snuck back into his bedroom.

The moon was still large.

He slept soundly.

The day of the test arrived at last. Gomer came downstairs.

Gideon was up already talking with Sylvia.

"Sylvia—you have GOT to stop leaving these cigarettes everywhere."

"I forgot," she said. And then. "Where's Gomer? I want to see him."

Gomer groaned. He so didn't have time for this. Gideon came out into the kitchen, and motioned at him.

Gomer sighed and walked into the den. It was filled from floor to ceiling with books, bags of books, and crates filled with papers.

"Hi Sylvia," he said.

"Why Gomer," said Sylvia—reclining in a yellow robe on her La-Z-Boy. "You're getting so big. You look just like your mother."

*I don't look anything like her,* thought Gomer.

"Gideon—get me some more coffee would you?" Gideon went out.

Sylvia beckoned to Gomer. He came over to her.

"Your mother is a wonderful person," said Sylvia. softly. "She left Narrow Interior because she had to follow her dreams. That's a good thing to do, and she just—well—she just couldn't handle your father."

She leaned over to Gomer. "He's very depressed," she said quietly.

"I know that," Gomer said.

Sylvia put her arms out and hugged him. She smelled of old roses –strangely sweet

"I understand," she said. "You have every right to be angry. But forgive yourself when the time comes. Forgive yourself for being so mad at them."

"I'm not mad," he said.

Mackie pounded on the kitchen door and they started walking. Mackie was silent for a good 10 minutes.

"Christopher isn't interested in me at all, is he?" she said as they got close to the gym.

Gomer thought about it.

"I don't think he is," he said. "By the way, I think I might be gay."

"Do you like him?"

"Yes."

Mackie was quiet for another 5 minutes.

"It's ok," she said. "Good luck on the test."

Direct, as always.

They got to the pool. They had class. Then it was time for Gomer and a couple of other Senior Lifesaving students to take the practical test.

"Let's start," said Birch.

"Wait," said Mackie. "We are waiting for Christopher. He's going to be one of the drowners."

"No he isn't," said Birch. He looked gruffer than usual if that was possible. "He's been arrested."

*The moped*, thought Gomer. *Someone saw him.*

"Breaking and entering," said one of the Senior Lifesaving boys. And someone whispered. "And he had a gun."

*He did?*

"Gomer—you're with me—" said the coach, and he dove in the water.

Gomer put his goggles on. He breathed.

He remembered practicing lifesaving with Christopher. He also thought—suddenly—of his mother. Who had left him, but who had also managed to save her own life.

Then he looked at Mackie, his friend, who liked him even though he was probably gay and even though the guy they both liked liked him better. At least for a little while.

He swam—not fast—but deliberately, and sized up the situation. The coach was acting the part of the classic desperate drowner, and as soon as Gomer approached, he grabbed him.

Desperate drowners are all the same.

Certainty arose in Gomer and that certainty planted Gomer's right foot into the drowner's solar plexus. Certainty pushed against that stomach hard and straightened that leg. The drowner doubled over, and at that moment Gomer grabbed him and dragged him to the end of the pool. And pulled him out.

Coach Birch coughed, swore, sat up.

"Now for the unconscious rescue and CPR part of the test," he said.

Gomer walked home alone with his Junior Lifeguard certification. Mackie stayed behind to talk with a girl who had just moved to town.

He felt ok. So ok, in fact that he didn't panic when he saw the fire trucks ringed around Sylvia's burning house.

Sylvia sat on her La-Z-Boy on the front lawn. She was talking to a paramedic.

Gideon was arguing with a firefighter about going back inside.

"I have to go get my paintings," he said.

"Too late," said the firefighter.

"Dad," said Gomer.

Gideon turned towards his son.

"I'm glad you weren't here, Buddy."

Gomer thought about telling him about the lifesaving test, but instead he took his father's hand.

"Dad—listen," he said. "I'm not your buddy. I'm your son."

Gideon looked at him. "It's just an expression."

Gomer was going to have to get clearer.

"Listen to me, Gideon," he said and this time he put both hands on both his father's arms. "I could get sick again. I NEED you. If you want to paint, paint. If not, find something else. Get help. Talk to someone. If you don't, I'm going to find someplace else to live. I'm going to…. emancipate."

"I'm scared," Gideon said.

"Me too," said Gomer. "Deal with it."

Gomer walked away and watched the fire.

The curtains burst into flame and the flame was so thick and red and bright it looked like water. A firefighter stood there blasting his hose. And in the arc of water, Gomer saw the woman in the grey dress, Molly, and the man, Bernhard. There were others with them, dancing in and out of the droplets.

*This is how we died*, Molly called out to him over the noise. *Burned because we worshipped the light in our own way.* Then she and Bernhard faded and Gomer saw Christopher playing the mandolin as the Dankers performed a play in the meeting house. They held large dolls that they used like puppets. Then Christopher kissed him in the municipal pool that was also a forest that was also a street that was also a river that led all the way to China.

"I'm so sorry about your house," said someone to him. Gomer turned and saw it was Henry Holbein, the billionaire neighbor from the television. The one who had been in the fight.

"Did you see what was in the water?" said Gomer.

Henry squinted at the water from the hose, cocked his head. He smiled.

"That's why I'm here," he said. "I've come to restore the Danker meetinghouse and put on the play. Molly is my ancestor. The founder of the Dankers, who were Anabaptists. Believers in adult baptism."

"Hey, you—" said a tall guy in his yellow firefighting gear. "I managed to save these." He handed Gomer a box.

Gomer opened up the box and there were the knockoff Barbie and the GI Joe—and a new toy he had not seen before.

It was a rubber turtle.

"Isn't that Gamera—the fighting turtle?" said Henry Holbein. "I used to watch him on tv. Born of radioactivity!"

"According to Korean tradition, the turtle is a symbol of courage and long life," the firefighter said.

Gomer took a closer look at the firefighter. He was very young. He looked, just a little, like Jacob might have, if he had lived.

"I've had radiation," said Gomer to Henry Holbein and the firefighter.

"Dude—then, you must be really strong," the firefighter said.

They watched as the young firefighter went back with the others, working the hoses to douse the flames.

# About the Author

**Stephanie Barbé Hammer** is a 6-time Pushcart Prize nominee in fiction, nonfiction and poetry with work published in *The Bellevue Literary Review, Hayden's Ferry Review, Pearl, the James Franco Review, Isthmus, Cafe Irreal,* and *the Gold Man Review.*

She is the author of the prose poem chapbook SEX WITH BUILDINGS (dancing girl press), the full-length collection HOW FORMAL? (Spout Hill Press), the fabulist novel THE PUPPET TURNERS OF NARROW INTERIOR (Urban Farmhouse Press), and the craft of writing magical realism manual, DELICIOUS STRANGENESS (Spout Hill Press).

Originally from Manhattan, Stephanie lived in Southern California for 30 years. She is managing editor of SHARK REEF Literary Magazine and sits on the advisory board of WRITERS BLOC Los Angeles.

BAMBOO DART PRESS

112 N. Harvard Ave. #65
Claremont, CA 91711
chapbooks@bamboodartpress.com
www.bamboodartpress.com

www.ingramcontent.com/pod-product-compliance
Lightning Source LLC
Chambersburg PA
CBHW080756120626
46557CB00006B/1289